Lucy's Lab

Solids, Liquids, Guess Who's Got Gas

Lucy's Lab

Solids, Liquids, Guess Who's Got Gas?

by Michelle Houts
Illustrated by Elizabeth Zechel

Sky Pony Press
New York

First Edition

Sky Pony Press books may be purchased in bulk at special discounts for sales promotion, corporate gifts, fund-raising, or educational purposes. Special editions can also be created to specifications. For details, contact the Special Sales Department, Sky Pony Press, 307 West 36th Street, 11th Floor, New York, NY 10018 or info@skyhorsepublishing.com.

Visit our website at www.skyponypress.com
Books, authors, and more at www.skyponypressblog.com

www.michellehouts.com
www.elizabethzechel.com

10 9 8 7 6 5 4 3 2 1

Library of Congress Cataloging-in-Publication Data

Names: Houts, Michelle, author. | Zechel, Elizabeth, illustrator.
Title: Solids, liquids, guess who's got gas / Michelle Houts ; illustrated by Elizabeth Zechel.
Other titles: Solids, liquids, guess who's got gas
Description: First edition. | New York : Sky Pony Press, [2017]. | Series: Lucy's lab ; 2 | Summary: Lucy learns all about states of matter, and a school field trip and the Fall Harvest Festival gives her the chance to put her new knowledge to good use.
Identifiers: LCCN 2017008966| ISBN 9781510710672 (hardback) | ISBN 9781510710689 (paperback) | ISBN 9781510710696 (ebook)
Subjects: | CYAC: Matter—Properties—Fiction. | Harvest festivals—Fiction. | School field trips—Fiction. | Schools—Fiction. | BISAC: JUVENILE FICTION / Science & Technology. | JUVENILE FICTION / Readers / Chapter Books. | JUVENILE FICTION / School & Education. | JUVENILE FICTION / Girls & Women.
Classification: LCC PZ7.H8235 Sol 2017 | DDC [Fic]--dc23 LC record available at https://lccn.loc.gov/2017008966

Cover illustration by Elizabeth Zechel
Cover design by Sammy Yuen

Printed in Canada

Contents

GRANITE CITY
ELEMENTARY SCHOOL
HAR

Chapter One

Names

The sign in front of Granite City Elementary school used to say WELCOME BACK, STUDENTS AND STAFF! But today, all it says is HAR.

From my seat in Room 2-C, I can see Mr. Farmer out there looking through a box for more letters.

Once, when I was in first grade, I asked my dad why a farmer worked at my school. He told me that Mr. Farmer isn't a farmer. He's a custodian. Then Dad told me that a long time ago, before people had two names, if there were two people named John, they'd call one John the Baker and the other John the Farmer. So lots of people have last names that are jobs.

In my second grade class, there's Collin Cook. I bet his great-great-great-great grandfather was a cook. Maybe even for someone famous. And there's Natalie Shoemaker. Once, I read a story about a man who made shoes and had elves who helped him in the night while he slept.

Mr. Farmer has added a *V* to the sign, so now it says HARV. I'm guessing he's putting the name *Harvey* up there, but I have no idea why. I don't know anyone named Harvey.

Some of us in Room 2-C don't have jobs for last names. Like me. I'm Lucinda Marie Watkins. Everyone calls me Lucy, and I have never even asked what a Watkins is.

And, there's Miss Flippo. I have no clue what a Flippo is, but it sounds kind of like a clown. I would never, ever, ever tell Miss Flippo that, though. She's the best and smartest teacher I've ever had.

Right now, Miss Flippo is writing this week's spelling words on the whiteboard, and we're supposed to copy them down in our spelling journals. You might be worried that I'm not paying attention, but it's okay. I can listen and think at the same time.

Mom calls me a good multitasker. It's a good thing I'm a good multitasker, because Mr. Farmer has added an *E* to the sign, and I'm not going to stop looking out that window until I know who this Harvey person is and why he's important enough to get his name on the school sign.

"Three minutes until recess, class," Miss Flippo announces.

I hurry to get the last six spelling words written into my journal. I never want to miss recess, especially when it's outside. Outside is my favorite place to be. That's because outside is where nature is. And

nature is fascinating.

The bell rings just as I get the very last word down.

Behind me, my best friend and only cousin, Cora, leaps out of her seat. Her pink tutu skirt flits and flounces as we speed-walk to recess. We always follow the "No

Running" rule.

"I can't wait!" she says. "What are you going to be?"

"Be?" I ask. "Cora, what are you talking about?"

Cora sighs. "Lucy, I'm talking about the best day ever!"

She points across the playground to the front of the school. Mr. Farmer steps back from the sign, picks up his box of letters, and heads toward the office.

Now the sign says: HARVEST FESTIVAL, OCTOBER 15TH.

That's much better than a visit from some guy named Harvey!

Chapter Two

The Worst Part of the Best Day

"What's a Harvest Festival?" Georgia from Alabama asks Cora and me, her swing whooshing past mine, and then past Cora's.

I had forgotten that since Georgia just moved here at the beginning of school, she doesn't know anything about Granite City Elementary School's biggest event of the year.

"It's a whole day of games—" I try to yell back to Georgia as her swing passes mine again.

"—and rides—" Cora adds.

Georgia whooshes by again. "I can't hear you!"

"—and food and—" I holler.

"What did you say?" Georgia yells over her shoulder.

Whoosh!

This is not working. "STOP!"

I plant both feet in the gray gravel and grind my swing to a halt.

Georgia does the same. Cora taps her feet lightly on the stones, taking three passes to slow down enough to stop. She's wearing her favorite pink shoes, and I know she would be sad if she got them all messed up in the gravel.

When we're all stopped, I say, "Okay, ready?"

Cora nods. Georgia from Alabama nods, too.

"On three. One. Two. Three!"

We all pull back on our chains and lift our feet at the very same time. At last! We're swinging together. Much better.

"The Harvest Festival is awesome!" Cora tells Georgia on our upswing.

"The whole town comes!" I say as we glide back.

Georgia is between us, and her head is turning left and then right to hear Cora and me.

"And you can win prizes!" Cora, up, tutu up. (It's a good thing she wears pink shorts under those tutu skirts.)

"And there's a Cake Walk." Me, back.

"And a contest for the best costume!" Cora, up.

Even though it's my turn, and Georgia is looking right at me, I don't say a word.

I don't like dressing up in costumes. I never know what to dress up as and every year, at the very last minute, my mother comes up from the basement with something that will turn me into something I didn't ask to be.

In Kindergarten, I went to the Harvest Festival as a mouse. I wore a gray sweat suit with felt ears and a long tail my mom made. In first grade, when Cora's mom, Aunt Darian, offered to make matching princess dresses for us, I told a little fib and said I already had a costume picked out, even though I didn't. That year, I was the most unoriginal farmer anyone had ever seen. Blue overalls, flannel shirt, straw hat, stuffed pig under one arm.

Whoosh!

Somehow, we've gotten out of rhythm again. Georgia's swing whizzes right by me.

"I said, what are you going to dress up as?" she calls over her shoulder.

I pass her on my way up.

"I don't know. But I'll think of something!"

Chapter Three

What's the Matter?

In the afternoon, Miss Flippo is waiting for us when we get back from art class.

The first thing I notice is that the Science Lab is all rearranged. I think we are the luckiest second graders on the whole planet, because Miss Flippo was an astronaut once, and she really did get to go to space. She calls us her "scientists," and we have a real Science Lab in our classroom.

Our first science unit was all about habitats. Miss Flippo let us change Room 2-C into a woodland forest, a desert, the Arctic, a rainforest, and an ocean. I was so happy to be in the desert group—even though awful Stewart Swinefest was also in it—because brown is my favorite color and there're so many different kinds of brown in the desert. But last week, we helped Miss Flippo take down all of the habitats, and she promised we'd love our new science unit just as much.

"Hurry to your seats," Miss Flippo says. "We have a lot to do this afternoon."

Stewart, sitting behind me on my right, groans and slouches in his seat. But I sit up straight and tall. I want Miss Flippo to know I'm ready to hear anything she has to tell us about science. It's my favorite subject in the world.

"Today, scientists," she says, "we're going to talk about matter."

Stewart sits up a little straighter. "What's the matter?" He snorts. "Get it? Matter?"

I roll my eyes at him, but he's too busy laughing at his own joke to see.

Miss Flippo smiles. "I knew someone would say that. But, it's actually the question of the day. What is matter?"

Natalie raises her hand, and Miss Flippo calls on her.

"Is it a problem?" Natalie asks.

Miss Flippo nods her head. "You mean, like when we say, 'What's the matter with Joe today?'"

"Yes, like that," Natalie replies.

"That's one way to use the word," Miss Flippo tells us. "But here's another way to think of matter."

Miss Flippo reaches into a large bag on her desk. It wasn't there before we left the classroom for art class, or I would have noticed.

"Tessa and Eddie, please give a cup to every student."

When Tessa and Eddie have finished passing out the cups, Miss Flippo reaches into her bag and pulls out two big bottles of root beer.

"I love root beer!" Manuel says, and most of us agree.

"Me, too!"

"It's my favorite!"

I love root beer, too. Root beer is another one of those wonderful brown things.

"Lucy," Miss Flippo says, "I'd like you and Gavin to very carefully pour some root beer into each cup."

I hurry to help, but once I start pouring, I slow down and take my time, so I don't spill any. Logan is the only one who doesn't want root beer. He says he only likes the taste of orange pop.

"Can we drink it now?" Stewart asks, almost before Gavin has finished pouring the last cup.

"Not yet," Miss Flippo says. While I was busying pouring, Miss Flippo had written three words on the whiteboard:

SOLID

LIQUID

GAS

"Look at what's in your cup," Miss Flippo says. "Is the root beer solid?" She holds her cup up and lets the root beer slosh around a little bit.

"No!" the class answers in unison.

"It's liquid!" Heather says.

"That's right." Miss Flippo nods. "Now, what shape is your root beer?"

Shape? I stare at the liquid in my cup. It's not a circle, even though my cup is round. It's definitely not a square. It's kind of . . .

"Cup-shaped!" Brody calls out the same answer I was thinking.

"Indeed. Liquid takes the shape of the container it's in."

Stewart has his face down over his cup, and the tip of his freckled nose is almost touching his root beer.

"Now?" he asks. "Now can we drink it?"

Miss Flippo smiles. "I think you'll want to wait for this next part, Stewart."

She reaches into her bag once more and produces a tub of vanilla ice cream and a round metal scoop.

Room 2-C goes wild!

"This ice cream has been in the freezer all day," she tells us. She takes off the lid and runs the metal scoop over the surface of the ice cream. I can tell she's pushing hard because she twists up her mouth and stands on her toes.

Miss Flippo carefully plops a perfect round ball of frozen ice cream into an empty cup and holds it up for all of us to see.

"I'll ask you the same question I asked about the root beer. Is this ice cream solid?"

I look at the ball of ice cream. Its shape is still round, even though the cup is—like Brody said—cup-shaped.

Almost everyone answers yes. But Ming and I are thinking the same thing.

"But it's soft," Ming says, and I nod.

"You're right," Miss Flippo says. "It *is* soft, but look at the shape. While it's still cold, it holds its own shape, right?"

Sure enough, the ice cream is still in a perfect ball.

"So it *is* a solid!" Ming decides.

"Yes, it's a solid. And being soft is another of its *properties*," Miss Flippo says.

Now Stewart isn't the only one getting antsy. Most of Room 2-C has figured out that Miss Flippo is giving us root beer floats, and we can't wait to eat them!

"*Now?*" Stewart cries.

Miss Flippo holds up one finger to tell him to be just a little more patient. "There's one more thing you need to see."

She carefully empties the cup with the

perfect solid ball of ice cream into her cup with liquid root beer and we all *ooh* when the fizz bubbles almost to the top.

"Where did all that foam come from?" Miss Flippo asks. "There were only two parts: root beer and ice cream. But now there are three."

Ajay raised his hand. "The foam came from the bubbles in the root beer."

"That's right, Ajay. Do you think there would be any foam if we added a scoop of ice cream to water?"

"No!" Room 2-C answers, all together.

"The bubbles in root beer, and in all pop, are actually air bubbles. And air is not a solid, right?"

"Right!"

"And air is not a liquid, right?"

"Right!"

Miss Flippo points to the three words on

the board. "So, air must be a—"

"Gas!"

Miss Flippo is beaming. "What smart second graders you are!" she exclaims.

Collin raises his hand.

"Collin?"

"We may be smart, but we're also starving! Can we have root beer floats now?"

Chapter Four

Back at the Lab

After school, Cousin Cora and I go straight to my lab.

It's actually my old playhouse, but after Miss Flippo showed me how cool it is to have a science lab, I took out all the toys that my little brother, Thomas, and I had put in there, and I added science-y stuff. Except Miss Flippo doesn't like the word *stuff*. She says it's not very specific, and *stuff* can be anything in the world.

Hmm. The new word we learned today—*matter*—is kind of *stuff*, except *matter* isn't anything in the world. It's *everything* in the world!

Cora is looking at all my specimens. I have to admit, I've started quite a collection since the beginning of the school year. I've got rocks and leaves and some pinecones from the park.

"Oh! What on earth happened to that gorgeous creature?" Cora cries, and I already know what she's talking about before I even look up.

It's a yellow, blue, and black Swallowtail butterfly that was already dead when I carefully peeled it off the grill of Dad's pickup truck. Right away I looked up what kind of butterfly it is. It's called a *Swallowtail* because the backs of its wings look the tail of a swallow. I didn't know what a swallow looked like, either, so I had to look that up next, and sure enough, a swallow is a bird that has a tail that looks just like this butterfly.

"Butterfly versus truck," I explain to Cora. "Truck won."

Cora uses one fingertip to stroke the butterfly's delicate wings. "That's *so* sad," she says.

"I know," I agree. "But at least now we can study it." I hand Cora the magnifying glass I borrowed from Mom's desk.

"Look at that!" Cora says, leaning close to the butterfly. "I thought it was just yellow and black with a little blue, but look. I see red, too. Do you?"

I don't see any red, but I look anyway when she passes me the magnifying glass. I move the glass up and down and all around until I zero in on the butterfly's tail. Or tails. It actually has two, one on each side of its middle. "Hey, you're right. I see a tiny bit of red on each of its tails."

Cora smiles.

"Good job, Cora! You are becoming a real scientist!"

"I never knew science could be so"—Cora twirls around, being dramatic—"so COLORFUL!"

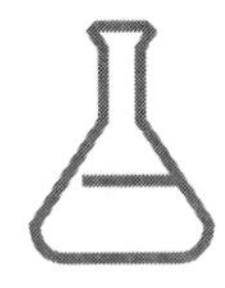

The library is open late on Tuesday evenings, which means Aunt Darian has to work late, and *that* means Cora gets to eat supper with us most Tuesdays. Tonight, Dad is trying out a new pasta recipe, and I know it'll be good because Dad's probably the best cook in Granite City.

"Are you girls getting excited about the Harvest Festival?" Mom asks as she passes the salad.

"Oh, yes!" Cora says. "Except, this year, I'm having trouble thinking of a costume."

"That's not like you, Cora," Mom says. "You usually come up with wonderful costumes."

Thomas passes the salad without taking any. "Just be a princess. Or a fairy. Or a fairy princess. That's what you usually do."

"Thomas, be polite." Dad reminds my little brother to use his manners.

"It's okay," Cora says. "He's right. But I was thinking about being something different this year."

Dad nods and passes a steaming bowl of bowtie pasta with creamy white sauce on top of it. "How about you, Lucy?"

"Sure, I'll have some!" I answer.

Dad laughs. "Well, of course you should have some pasta! I was just asking if you've given any thought to your Harvest Festival costume."

I frown. "No," I say, and it's kind of a lie. I've been thinking about the costume contest ever since Cora told Georgia about it at recess. I don't know why I don't like dressing up. I just don't.

"Well, there's time," Mom says with a smile and she plops a big spoonful of pasta on her plate.

Chapter Five

The Experiment

Mrs. James is the principal of Granite City Elementary School. She wears really big glasses that hide her big eyebrows until she's surprised, and then they pop up over the top of her glasses like two caterpillars.

This morning, Mrs. James is greeting students as they get off buses in front of the school. "Good morning, Lucy." Mrs. James smiles, her eyebrows hiding behind her glasses.

"Good morning, Mrs. James!" I answer. I start to walk right past her, but then I think about Mr. Farmer and Natalie Shoemaker again. I stop.

"Mrs. James?"

"Yes, Lucy?"

"Did you know that some people have jobs for last names?"

"I sure did, Lucy." Mrs. James nods. She's really smart. All principals are really smart, I think.

"Well, you don't. You actually have a first name for a last name."

Pop! Up come the caterpillar eyebrows. "And this is important because—?"

"Oh, no reason, really," I say. "I just thought you should know."

"Well, thank you, Lucy," says Mrs. James, but her voice doesn't sound very thankful at all.

SCHOOLS 21

When I get into Room 2-C, Stewart Swinefest is already there. Like usual, Stewart announces my arrival with a loud "Lucy Goosey is here!"

Collin and Brody laugh along with Stewart, but Annalisa says, "That's not very nice, Stewart."

I smile at her. She's usually very quiet. It's nice of her to stick up for me. "Thanks," I say, and she smiles back.

As soon as I hang up my jacket, Cora rushes over to me.

"Keep your jacket on," she says. "Miss Flippo says we're going outside for science today."

I love when we go outside for anything. But mostly for science, because that usually means we're doing an experiment.

Just then Miss Flippo comes into the room with a big box. "Room 2-C," she says. "As soon as everyone is here, and we've heard the morning announcements, we're going outdoors to conduct an experiment."

"But we don't have science in the morning," Collin pipes up.

"The weather forecast is for showers later today, so I want to be sure we get this done before it rains," Miss Flippo explains.

When the announcements are finished, we line up and walk quietly out to the playground.

"Let's make a circle right here on the basketball court," Miss Flippo suggests, still carrying the big box. "Have a seat, everyone."

Miss Flippo reaches into the box and takes out a plastic bag of balloons, ones that haven't been blown up yet. "I'll pass this bag around," she says, "and I'd like each of you to reach in and take one. And, remember, color doesn't matter. Just reach in and grab the first balloon you touch."

When the bag comes to me, I close my eyes and pull out a green balloon. I pass the bag to Cora and I see her close her eyes, too. Only, then she opens one eye just a squinty little bit and, sure enough, her hand comes out holding a pink balloon. She smiles at me and passes the bag on to Ming.

After everyone has a balloon, Miss Flippo asks, "Okay, scientists. What's inside your balloon?"

We all look at our floppy balloons. They sure look empty to me.

"Nothing," Gavin says.

"A tiny little bit of air?" Bridget guesses.

Miss Flippo nods. "Bridget is right. Since the balloon has an open end, some air is most certainly inside the balloon. But not much, right?"

We all nod.

"So, let's fill our balloons up with gas, shall we? Ready? Go!"

Some of the kids look around to see what others are doing, but I know just what Miss Flippo means. I put the green balloon to my mouth and start blowing. Soon, everyone is puffing air into their balloons. I'm glad I helped my dad blow up balloons for Thomas's fourth birthday party, but when I'm almost finished, I remember something—I don't know how to tie it!

Just as I'm wondering if anyone else knows how, Miss Flippo says, "When your balloon feels like it's full of gas, pinch the end shut with your fingers, but don't tie it."

Whew! Off the hook for now!

I notice that most of the other kids from Room 2-C are a little pink in the face after blowing up their balloons.

"You just used your bodies to transfer air from the atmosphere"—Miss Flippo moves her arms around her head to show us that she means all the air around us—"to the inside of your balloons. And that air is a gas. Actually, as it comes out of your lungs, it's several gases: nitrogen, oxygen, and carbon dioxide."

I am thinking about these new words Miss Flippo has just shared and how they might look if I tried to spell them when I hear a noise coming from across the circle. It's like the sound Thomas makes when he's eaten too many soup beans.

Stewart and Brody are giggling, and Stewart is holding his balloon behind his back with both hands.

Phssssst.

The noise comes again, only louder, and now all the boys, and even Bridget and Georgia, are laughing.

"Stewart," says Miss Flippo, and I'm sure he's in for a good scolding, maybe even a trip to Mrs. James's office. But, instead, Miss Flippo says, "Stewart is actually one step ahead of me. Everyone, I want you to let the gas escape from your balloons. You can do it slowly, as Stewart has demonstrated, or you can just let go and see what happens."

Suddenly, the air is filled with flying balloons and funny noises. We all laugh and I chase my balloon as it flies out of my hand

and zigzags across the basketball court.

Miss Flippo claps three times and we all run back to our spots.

"Now," she says. "Please put your empty balloon on the ground beside you. Then pass these very, very carefully." Miss Flippo reaches into her box again and passes a balloon to Jack, who passes it to Logan, who passes it Sarah. Miss Flippo keeps getting more balloons out of the box, and soon balloons are coming one by one around the circle. I can see that these balloons are already filled and tied, but it isn't until Ajay hands the first squishy balloon to me and I pass it on to Cora that I realize they don't have air in them. They're full of water! No wonder Miss Flippo wanted us to pass them so carefully!

"Okay," Miss Flippo says. "What's inside the balloons you're holding?"

"Water!" Carl answers.

"Liquid!" I correct him.

Carl frowns at me. "Water *is* a liquid."

"You're absolutely right, Carl," Miss Flippo agrees. "Water is a liquid."

Carl's frown turns into a big grin.

"And you're right, too, Lucy. There *is* some kind of liquid in the balloons."

Now it's my turn to smile really big.

"And since we can't see or taste the liquid in the balloon," Miss Flippo says, "we are guessing it's water. That's called a *hypothesis.* A hypothesis is a guess, but it's not just any guess," she tells us. "I like to call it a smart guess. It's based on facts we already know are true. Why did no one guess that the balloons are filled with coffee? Coffee is a liquid."

Ming raises her hand. "Coffee is dark and this liquid is light.

"Yeah, and coffee is usually hot, and this balloon is cool," Brody adds.

"Very good." Miss Flippo looks pleased. "My young scientists are making hypotheses based on what they already know. Now, the next step is to test our hypothesis. We need to find out if we're right. How are we going to test our hypothesis? How will we find out if these balloons are, indeed, filled with water?"

"Break them?" Heather asks.

Miss Flippo nods.

We all look at one another. Are we really allowed to break our water balloons?

"Go ahead. But no aiming at another person." Miss Flippo stands back a bit.

Logan is the first to stand up. “Ready? Set? Go!” His blue balloon hits the sidewalk and bursts, scattering water in all directions.

Brody runs his balloon down the basketball court and tries to make a basket, but the balloon breaks against the backboard and water showers down on him. Georgia drops hers in the grass seven times before it finally bursts. Natalie pokes a tiny hole in her balloon with her fingernails, and we watch as the water shoots out in a steady stream.

Cora and I play Balloon Toss with ours, daring to get farther and farther away from each other until, *splat!* Both balloons break on our shoes at the very same time.

When Miss Flippo claps us back to the circle, some of us are a little damp, but we all agree that we tested our hypothesis and we were right. The evidence showed that the balloons were filled with water.

"So," says Miss Flippo, "we've seen two states of matter. What's another state of matter?"

"Solid?" Tessa answers.

I know Tessa's right, but I can't imagine how to fill a balloon with something solid.

Miss Flippo opens the box one last time. "Form a line and take a balloon. Then find a partner and discuss what you know about solids."

When it's my turn to reach into the box,

I pick up a yellow balloon and, right away, I know. These water balloons are frozen!

"Cold, cold, cold!" Ajay says, tossing his balloon from hand to hand.

"Lucy!" calls Georgia. "Be my partner!"

Georgia and I sit in the grass and drop our frozen balloons between us. It feels good to get mine out of my cold hands. I rub my palms together to warm them up.

"This is fun!" Georgia is almost squealing with excitement. "Mrs. Whittingham at my old school never took us outside for science!"

We stare at our frozen balloons. I poke mine. "Well, it certainly is solid," I say.

"Yep, hard as a rock," Georgia agrees.

I pick mine up again, but this time I pinch the tied end between my thumb and forefinger so I don't have to touch the coldest part of the balloon. "It's heavy, too.

Heavier than the liquid or gas balloons."

"I suppose there's frozen water inside," Georgia says.

"You mean you *hypothesize*," I say.

"Yeah, that's what I mean," Georgia says.

Just then, Miss Flippo's voice is louder than all the others and we all stop talking to listen.

"Okay, scientists," she says. "You may investigate the inside of your solid balloons.

You may do this any way you choose, but you may not throw them. I have some tools here that you may choose to use to conduct your research."

Stewart groans about not being allowed to throw his balloon, and he and Collin begin to plot other ways set off their ice bombs.

Georgia and I check out the tools Miss Flippo has collected for us. Georgia chooses a pair of scissors and I think that's a great idea.

We take turns cutting the balloons open and peeling them off the small round ball of ice.

"My ice is kind of cloudy," I say. "But there are some clear spots, too."

"Hey, look!" Georgia says. "I think there's something inside mine."

We both examine it and, sure enough, there's a colorful spot in the middle of

Georgia's ball of ice.

"Look at yours!" Georgia cries.

"Hey, mine has something in it, too!" I say.

All around us, others are discovering the same thing.

"So you have a solid," Miss Flippo says, "with something inside of it. How can you get that something out?"

"Melt the ice!" Brody shouts. He and Manuel lean over and start breathing warm air on their frozen spheres.

"That will take forever," Carl moans. He and Logan stand up and drop theirs from waist-high onto the blacktop basketball court. Carl's crumbles and the wing of a yellow plastic airplane appears.

"Cool!" Logan says, and soon we're all standing on the basketball court, dropping solid spheres until they shatter.

Georgia finds a red plastic gem in hers, and mine breaks into six pieces before I discover a small blue marble.

Cora has a quarter and Sarah has a seashell. Manuel finds a car inside his. Stewart finds a plastic T-Rex, which right away tries to eat Gavin's dog.

Suddenly, a gust of wind sweeps over the basketball court, and I feel a drop of rain.

"Room 2-C," says Miss Flippo, "we can finish indoors. Please gather every last balloon you see lying on the ground. Let's leave nothing behind except the chunks of ice, which will melt. And let's move quickly!"

More big drops plop down on us as we grab everything and hurry indoors.

Back inside Room 2-C, we work quietly at our desks, filling in a worksheet about solids, liquids, and gases, and recording our findings in our science journals. I roll my marble in my left hand while I write. It's only ten o'clock in the morning, but I'm pretty sure this day can't get any better.

WHAT'S the MATTER?

Write solid, liquid, or gas next to each word.

Apple

Lemonade

Crayon

Ball

Milk

Wind

Ice

Coffee

Rock

Ink

Name

Chapter Six

A Trip to the Library

Well, I was totally wrong about the day not getting any better. Right after lunch, Miss Flippo claps us to attention.

"I have an announcement," she says. "Usually, second graders do not take a fall field trip. We have a lot of excitement with the Harvest Festival just around the corner. This year, however, Mr. Weaver has invited us to visit his apple orchard, and since this is the perfect time of year to witness apple harvest, I couldn't turn him down."

Room 2-C cheers! Who doesn't love a field trip?

"So," Miss Flippo continues, "I'll be handing out permission slips and you'll need to get them signed and returned very quickly. Our trip is next Monday morning."

Miss Flippo keeps talking, but my brain is stuck on Mr. Weaver. I wonder how a family of weavers turned out to be apple farmers. I'll have to ask him when I get a chance.

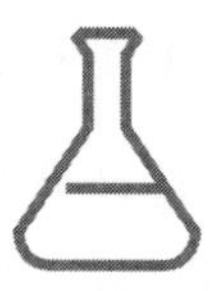

When I get off the bus at home, Dad is unloading tools from the back of his pick-up truck. He's a landscaper and he's very busy now with the leaves starting to fall in everyone's yards. Still, he picks up Thomas from preschool and is always home with us after school. Mom teaches at the university and she's usually home by suppertime.

"Dad, can I ride my bike to the library with Cora?" I ask.

"Homework?" he asks.

"Only spelling words," I say. "Cora and I can practice at the library."

"All right," Dad agrees. "In a month, it'll be too cold for bikes, so you may as well ride while you can. Don't forget your helmet."

"I know," I answer. Cora's house is only three blocks away, and the library, where Aunt Darian works, is right behind it. I always wear my helmet and stay on the sidewalk, so my parents let me go there by myself.

I swing my backpack over my shoulders and tighten the chin strap of my helmet. The air is getting cooler and I can tell fall is really here. I like all the seasons, but I think fall is my favorite.

As I pedal past houses, I notice the trees. Most still have green leaves, but some are starting to turn bright pinkish-yellow, like

the peel of a grapefruit. One day last week, Thomas was talking about the "grapefruit trees" on our street.

"Grapefruit trees don't grow in Granite City," I told him. "They grow in Florida."

But Thomas had insisted that he'd seen grapefruit trees. Now, as I pedal toward Cora's house, I'm pretty sure I'm looking at Thomas's "grapefruit" trees.

"I'm ready!" Cora calls to me when she sees me from a block away.

I don't even have to slow down as I pass her driveway. She just rides right along beside me and we make the turn toward the library. When we get there, we park our bikes and hang our helmets on the handlebars.

"Hello, girls!" Aunt Darian whispers when she sees us walk in.

"Mom, you have to sign this now," Cora says. She pulls the apple orchard field trip permission slip out of her backpack.

"Please?" Aunt Darian corrects Cora. 'Mom, would you *please* sign this?' is what you really meant to say, right?"

Cora and I giggle and Cora nods. "Yes, Mom. That's what I meant."

Aunt Darian looks over the form. "Oh, Mr. Weaver is so nice to invite you kids out

to the orchard. You'll love it there! Your mom and I used to go apple picking there when we were young, Lucy."

Aunt Darian signs the form and hands it back to Cora. "Now, what can I help you two find today?"

"Oh, I could use a new Princess Purple Power book," Cora says.

"Easy enough," says Aunt Darian. "What about you, Lucy?"

"Well, I'm thinking about the states of matter a lot these days."

"Also easy enough," says Aunt Darian. "I can point you in the right direction."

Then I remember that I promised Dad I'd study spelling words with Cora. Cora only protests a little, but she and I have to take the same spelling test on Friday, so she agrees and we head over to the Talking Room.

The library has study rooms—most of them Quiet Only rooms. But there's also one Talking Room, where we can use our real voices and we don't have to whisper.

This week's words aren't too hard and after fifteen minutes, Cora and I are feeling good about Friday's spelling test. She heads to the fiction section and I stop at the Circulation Desk to see what Aunt Darian has to say. She's on her computer.

"Here's what I've got, Lucy," she says. "In the juvenile nonfiction section, you'll find three books on the states of matter."

She hands me a slip of paper with the books' call numbers written on it. "Thanks," I say.

"And," she continues, "in the biographies, you'll find a book on this guy." She motions me over to her computer screen. There's a picture of a smart-looking man wearing glasses and holding a book. His necktie looks more like a scarf, but I can tell it's a very old picture, so maybe that's how men wore their ties back then.

Aunt Darian jots down his name for me and off I head to the nonfiction section. I get the books about states of matter and I read a lot of the same things Miss Flippo has taught us about solids, liquids, and gases. When I get to the third book, I'm very confused.

This book talks about *four* states of matter, not three. I decide to check it out and take it home to read, but before I go back to the Circulation Desk, I stop over in the biography section. The name Aunt Darian wrote down for me is Irving Langmuir, and it doesn't take me long to find his biography. He's on the front cover in the same scarf-tie and glasses, holding a book, and looking very serious. I add it to my pile and I'm off.

On the short bike ride back to Cora's house, Cora mentions the Harvest Festival costume contest again. With all the exciting science experiments and the news of the field trip, I had forgotten all about it. "I thought about dressing as Princess Purple Power," she says. "But I don't know. Ugh! I just don't know what to be this year, Lucy!"

"Maybe I'll be Lucy Watkins," I say, mostly joking.

"You can't be *you*!" Cora cries. Then her face brightens with an idea. "Hey, maybe I'll be you!"

"Right," I tell her. "You be me, and . . ."

". . . you can be *me*!" Cora finishes.

We get to her driveway, and it's a good thing, because we're both laughing so hard, we might fall off our bikes if we keep riding. Suddenly, Cora gets very serious.

"If I were you, I'd have to wear plain clothes," she says.

"*Normal* clothes," I correct her. "And if I were you, I'd have to wear a pink tutu."

"Or purple," Cora corrects me.

We both stand there for a minute.

"Let's think of something better," Cora suggests.

"Sounds good to me," I agree, and I pedal off toward home, feeling relieved that I don't have to wear a tutu. But I'm still no closer to having a costume for the Harvest Festival than I was before.

Chapter Seven

A Shocking Discovery

At supper, Mom says she remembers going to Mr. Weaver's apple orchard with Aunt Darian when they were little girls. "Oh, yes! It was so much fun. The cider press was going and the bees buzzed around, loving the juicy bits of smashed apple." She signs my permission slip and I put it safely into my backpack.

"Would you like to play a game after your shower?" Mom asks.

"No, I think I'll read my new library books," I say.

Mom grins. "That's my girl!"

Insects

In my room, I spread the new books out on the bed. I start with the one about the four states of matter. *Four?* Miss Flippo can't be wrong! She's the smartest person I've ever met.

But, sure enough, I read about solids, then liquids, then gases. And then, *plasma.* The book says plasma is in lightning and in television screens. It says we'd have a hard time living without plasma. How could Miss Flippo not know about plasma if it's so important?

Next, I read a little bit from the biography of Irving Langmuir. Except it's really written for people older than me, so I don't understand much of it, except that he was a guy who studied plasma. Soon, my eyes get heavy. By the time I crawl under the covers, I know two things: Miss Flippo doesn't know about plasma, and Irving Langmuir did.

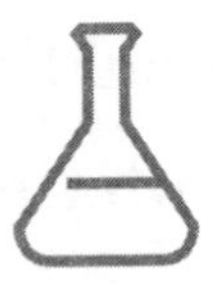

On Friday, it rains almost all day, so we have indoor recess. Miss Flippo opens the Science Lab for more solids, liquids, and gases experiments. She made some strange goopy stuff at home and brought it in for us to observe.

"Touch it, squeeze it, roll it, pour it. Do anything you possibly can with it, and then write down whether you think it's a liquid or a solid," Miss Flippo tells us as she puts lab coats on the four stools at the Science Lab. "Four at a time, please."

When the recess bell rings, Bridget and I are the first to the Science Lab. "We played with this stuff in first grade," Bridget says. "It's awesome."

We put on lab coats and Heather and Logan join us.

I've never seen the odd green goo before, but I can tell it's a liquid just by looking at in the bowl.

Miss Flippo comes over to get us started. "Are you ready?" she asks.

All four of us nod. She pours a puddle of it right in the center of the lab table. "There you go. Begin your observation," she says and then she walks away.

Bridget digs in with both hands. Heather touches the green puddle with one finger. Logan scoops up some with his left hand.

I just watch. The stuff oozes over Bridget's hand and dribbles back to the tabletop. *Yep, liquid. Definitely liquid.*

"Here, Lucy," says Logan. "Take this." I look, and Logan has rolled some of this liquid goo into a ball the size of a golf ball. I stare at it in his hand as he rolls and rolls and rolls it like play-dough.

"How did you do that, Logan?" I ask. "You can't roll a liquid into a ball."

Logan laughs. "It's not a liquid, Lucy. It's a solid. See?" He keeps rolling it and then holds it up. "Take it."

I put my hand flat out and Logan places the ball onto my palm. For a moment, it keeps its sphere shape. Then, suddenly, without any warning, it "melts" into my hand and I'm holding a handful of goo. Oozing, dripping slimy goo.

"Whoa!" Heather says. "Did you guys see that?"

Now I have to try to reform this liquid into the solid Logan had handed me. I squeeze my fingers shut tight and goo oozes between them. But when I open them, I have a solid chunk of matter resting in my palm.

"Now, roll it!" Logan says. "Hurry!"

Before the solid goo can melt again, I start to roll, like I do when Grandma visits from Ohio and we make cake balls. Sure enough, as long as I'm rolling, I can make a solid sphere that keeps its shape. But as soon as I stop, it collapses into liquid again.

Miss Flippo comes back. "Well, scientists, what do you think about this green goo? Liquid or solid?"

Bridget holds up two green hands, dripping with goo. "Liquid," she says.

Heather, who has been rolling a perfect golf-ball-sized sphere of goo, stops to show what she's made. "Solid," she says, but her solid quickly starts to lose its shape. "No, liquid," she changes her mind and starts rolling frantically. "Now, solid again!" she announces.

"It's both," I say. "It's liquid when it's just resting on the table or in your hand. But it can turn solid when . . ." I don't know how to say what I want to say next.

". . . when pressure is applied." Miss Flippo finishes, helping me out.

"Yes! When pressure is applied!"

The recess bell rings. It's time for music, but there's a lot of goo mess on the table.

"Miss Flippo, may I stay here for a minute and help you clean up?" I ask.

"Why, certainly, Lucy. I would appreciate that."

My lab partners wipe the goo off their fingers with a damp cloth and hurry to line up at the door for music. I scoop goo back into the bowl and decide I have to tell Miss Flippo what I learned in the library book.

"Miss Flippo?" I say.

"Yes, Lucy?"

"You said there are three states of matter, right?"

Miss Flippo smiles like she already knows what I'm going to say. "Well, I did say that almost everything we come into contact with daily is either a solid, a liquid, or a gas."

"I found out that you're forgetting one," I say. I hope she doesn't feel too badly. After all, she was smart enough to be an Educator Astronaut a few years ago. She might be embarrassed about this.

"Oh? Which one?" she asks. "Because there are several more. Let's see, there are—"

What Miss Flippo says next, I can't even tell you. It's a long list of crystal this and spinning that and super solid something. When she's done, she says,

"Oh, and of course, there's plasma. Could that be the one you're thinking of?"

I just nod.

"I'm so proud of you, Lucy! At the science teachers' conference I attended last summer, we looked at the newest science text books, and they all include four states of matter, not three, in the second grade editions."

I think I'm still nodding when Miss Flippo says, "Well, I think we're all cleaned up here. Are you ready for music?"

"Yes," I croak, finding my voice and heading for the door.

"Oh, Lucy," I hear Miss Flippo say. "I should ask you, how did you find out about plasma?"

"From Irving Langmuir," I manage to say.

Miss Flippo is beaming. "Well, then! Since Irving Langmuir told you about plasma, would you mind if I asked you to tell your classmates what you've learned?"

"I don't mind at all," I say, because I've not only got my voice, but I've also got a fantastic idea.

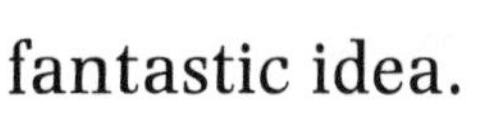

Chapter Eight

A Lesson Learned

It rains all weekend, and Sunday evening Mom says, "Lucy, it's not looking good for your field trip in the morning."

But when Monday morning comes, the sun gets up just at the same time I do. I get dressed in jeans and a sweatshirt, and Mom reminds me to wear my oldest sneakers because it's bound to be muddy in the orchard.

Mrs. James waves us into the school, and Miss Flippo takes attendance and asks me to tell the class about plasma and Irving Langmuir. They don't look very interested and suddenly I understand why Miss Flippo is always using experiments and activities to teach us new things. When I get to the part about lightning and televisions, a few of the kids get a little more interested.

"We saw the plasma TVs at the store," Ajay says.

"My Uncle Dave got struck by lightning once, and he's still alive!" Brody adds.

"Your Uncle Dave is a lucky man, Brody," Miss Flippo says. Then she gives last-minute instructions before we get on the bus for our trip.

"You've learned a lot about three—now four—states of matter since we started this science unit," she tells us. "Today, I want you to listen to Mr. Weaver and learn about the apple trees and apples, but all the while, I'd like you to try to identify the solids, liquids, and gases around us. Hopefully, there will be no lightning, so it's unlikely we'll find any electrically charged gases or plasma around us. Ready, everyone?"

Room 2-C is more than ready. We pile onto the bus and look out the windows at the brown farm fields as we leave Granite City. Some fields still have corn standing in them. Their dried-out stalks are leaning and their long leaves look like arms dragging

on the ground. Other fields are already harvested and we just see brown dirt. In one field, a farmer—not Mr. Farmer the custodian but a real farmer—is driving a huge combine through the corn, knocking it down and into the belly of the machine.

Mr. Weaver's orchard isn't too far away, and soon we're walking down a long row of apple trees, listening to Mr. Weaver talk. "Many of the apples were picked in September," he tells us, "but we're still picking the later varieties."

We come to a place where a dozen men and women are on ladders. They've got big bags hanging across their bodies and they are picking apples and placing them gently in the bags.

I think about the corn-harvesting machine, and I raise my hand.

"Lucy, do you have a question for Mr. Weaver?" Miss Flippo asks.

"Yes. Mr. Weaver, why don't you have a machine that picks apples?"

Mr. Weaver nods. "That would be wonderful, but apples are a delicate fruit. They bruise, just like you and me. Humans have to handle the apples carefully enough not to bruise them when they're picked."

Stewart Swinefest seems to always be at the back of the group. Once, when I turn around, I see him reach up and pick an apple off a tree then take a big bite.

"Stewart!" I whisper. "You're not supposed to do that!"

He sticks his tongue out at me and says, "Be quiet, Lucy Goosey. You're not supposed to be talking."

As we pass through the orchard, I see Stewart pick and chomp on another apple and then another and then another.

Next, we go into a big barn, where people are sorting the apples.

The best

apples go into one bin and the small or oddly shaped ones go into another. The "oddballs," as Mr. Weaver calls them, get picked up by a forklift and moved into the next room. There, two men are operating an old-fashioned cider press. The apples go in, then they get squeezed between two big, wooden blocks with a trough dug out of the middle, and then the cider pours down into a bucket.

"Liquid!" whispers Tessa, pointing to the cider, and I nod. She's right. The machine is turning solid apples into liquid cider!

The whole class moves on, but behind me I hear chewing. It's Stewart, of course. He's pulling apples from his pockets and chowing down as fast as he can.

"Hush your mouth, Lucy Goosey," he says, running past me to catch up with the class. I didn't even say anything!

At the end of the tour, we get to taste apple cider, and Mr. Weaver's grown-up daughter spreads homemade apple butter on pieces of white bread for everyone.

When we're lining up for the bus, we all shake Mr. Weaver's hand and I get my chance to ask him about his name.

"Did your ancestors weave fabric?" I ask.

Mr. Weaver looks a little surprised.

"I've had a lot of visitors, young lady, but you're the first to ask that question." He thinks for a few seconds. "I can't actually say that I know the answer, but I do know they came to the United States from Switzerland. Back as far as I can trace my family, we've always been farmers."

"Thank you, Mr. Weaver," I say, and I climb on the bus. When I slide into a seat with Cora, I hear munching noises behind me. It's Stewart. Of course it's Stewart.

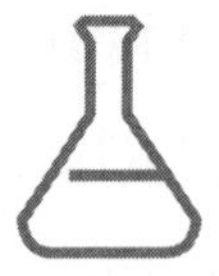

Back at Granite City Elementary, we go straight to lunch and then afternoon recess, and then, finally, back to Room 2-C.

"Let's talk about our trip this morning and how it relates to what we've learned about states of matter," Miss Flippo says.

"The trees were solid," Logan says.

"The apples were solid," Natalie adds.

"The barns and buildings were solid," Manuel says.

"The ladders and bins were solid, too," says Eddie.

Miss Flippo agrees. "And what did you see today that could be considered a liquid?"

"The cider!" Tessa and a dozen others all say at once.

"And maybe the apple butter, too?" Annalisa asks.

"No," Carl disagrees. "The apple butter was thick. The lady used a spoon to spread it on the bread."

"Ah, then, we'd better go back to the beginning to figure this out," Miss Flippo says. She pulls up our definitions from the first day of our unit and reads, "Liquid takes the shape of the container it's in."

"So," I say, "the apple butter is a liquid, because when it's in the jar, it fills up the shape of the jar."

"That's correct. It's a thick liquid, but it's a liquid."

I realize there's one voice I'm used to hearing almost constantly, but I haven't heard it once since we got back to the classroom. I look back and to my right and Stewart is slouched down in his seat. Both arms are folded across his stomach.

Miss Flippo is asking the class about gases. Room 2-C is silent.

Suddenly Collin blurts out, "The air!"

Miss Flippo nods. "Yes, of course. We always count on the air around us to contain the many gases we need for breathing. Anything else?"

Liquids are easy. Solids are easy. But gases are harder. The whole room is quiet.

So very quiet.

Until . . .

Phssssst.

And again, only louder, *Phhsssssstt!*

All eyes turn to Stewart Swinefest. I bet he has a balloon under his desk that he's letting the air out of a little at a time.

But he's still sitting the same way he was a minute ago, with his arms folded across his belly. His face looks a little green. Sarah and Eddie, who sit on either side of him, begin to scoot their desks away.

"Miss Flippo," Stewart moans. "I don't feel so good."

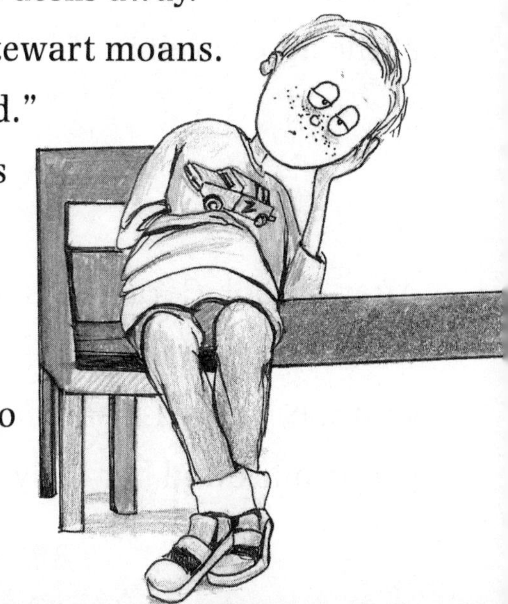

Miss Flippo leaps to her feet and walks Stewart into the hallway. When she comes back into the room alone, she dials the office and lets the nurse know Stewart's on his way to the clinic.

"He ate a lot of apples," I tell Miss Flippo. "I mean *a lot* of apples." I'm usually not a tattletale, but I think Miss Flippo should know. I guess she thinks it's important, too, because she tells the nurse before she hangs up the phone.

"Apples, my young scientists," she says, "are full of fiber and natural sugars, both of which can cause a lot of gas when eaten in excess. I think we've just answered our question about what kind of gases we found at the apple orchard!"

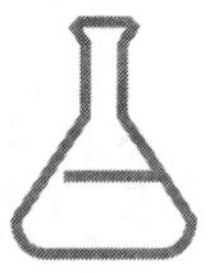

After school, Cora meets me in my lab.

"When winter comes, are we going to use your lab, Lucy? I mean, *brrr*!" Cora wraps her arm around her body and shivers.

"Maybe not every day," I say. "But an ice lab sounds fun, doesn't it?"

Cora doesn't look convinced. "Maybe," she says.

We talk about the excitement of the day and look at my specimens again. Cora still really likes the Swallowtail butterfly I collected.

"Are you ready for the Harvest Festival?" she asks.

That question would have really bugged me just a few days ago, but now I can answer with confidence. "Yes! What about you?"

I'm surprised when Cora doesn't even hesitate. "You bet!"

Chapter Nine

The Harvest Festival

"Are you sure about this, Lucy?" Dad asks. He takes a step back to stand with Mom and Thomas.

"I sure am," I answer.

"She's a man!" Thomas says.

Mom laughs. "Even I can't believe how great your Harvest Festival costume turned out this year! But, Lucy, are you prepared for the fact that many people won't know who you're supposed to be?"

"Yes, Mom," I say. "Nobody knows Irving Langmuir!"

With my dad's suit coat, a scarf-tie, and my hair under an old hat Mom found at the resale shop, I look just like the picture of the scientist who studied plasma. And I couldn't be happier!

"Well, let's go, then," Dad says, and we pile into his pickup truck for Granite City Elementary School.

The parking lot is already full of cars when we get there.

"It looks like all of Granite City has shown up for the Harvest Festival," Mom says.

"I want to win a cake. A whole cake!" Thomas squeals. He's finally old enough to remember last year's festival, where he really did win a double layer chocolate cake in the Cake Walk.

Inside, I look everywhere for Cora, except I don't know who—or what—I'm looking for. I should have begged her to tell me what costume she'd decided on.

I look in the gym where the games are set up. I look in the music room where the Cake Walk is, and I see Thomas is already standing on his lucky number four, waiting for the music to start.

In the hallway, I pass Miss Flippo.

"Hello, Mr. Langmuir," she smiles. "I'm awfully pleased to make your acquaintance. I've been a fan since college." Miss Flippo keeps a straight face and shakes my hand, and then we both burst out laughing. I wish my mom were standing right here to see that someone really did know who I was supposed to be.

“Have you seen Cora?” I ask.

“Oh, yes, indeed. She just flew by here a moment ago. She went that way.” Miss Flippo motions toward the cafeteria.

“Thanks!” I say as I hurry off. I can’t wait to see Cora.

The cafeteria is where all the yummy food is. Not cafeteria food today, though. Today it’s brownies and chili soup and hot dogs and caramel apples. It seems like everyone is trying to get into the cafeteria!

Right in front of me is a big black, yellow, and blue butterfly with wings so big they block the door. It looks like a Swallowtail, and I’m just thinking how much Cora would love that costume when the butterfly turns around.

“Cora!” I say. “That is the perfect costume for you!”

Cora the Swallowtail stares at me blankly. “Lucy? Is that you?”

"Yep, it's me! Well, actually I'm Irving Langmuir," I say.

"Irving who?" Cora asks.

"I'll explain later," I tell her, and we push her wings through the cafeteria doors.

Georgia comes rushing over to us, dressed in blue scrubs and looking more like a surgeon than our new friend from Alabama. "Lucy! Cora!" she squeals. "You were right. This *is* the best day of the whole year!"

"Outta my way, folks!" Stewart Swinefest swaggers in wearing cowboy boots and a big cowboy hat sitting down over his eyes. He has a sheriff's badge on his shirt, and he comes right over to us.

"Pardon me, doc," he says to Georgia. "You're breaking the law here, butterfly." He looks from Cora to me. And then he bursts out laughing. "Lucy, who are you supposed to be? I thought for sure you'd be a goosey!"

I wonder if Stewart Swinefest knows his last name means "pig party." I almost tell him, but I decide to ignore him instead.

"Come on, girls," I say. "Let's go get some *apple cider.*"

About the Author

Michelle Houts is the award-winning author of several books for young readers. She lives on a farm with a farmer, some cattle, goats, pigs, and a Great Pyrenees named Hercules. She writes in a restored one-room schoolhouse. As a second-grader, Michelle begged her parents for a chemistry kit but wasn't quite sure what to do when she actually got it. Lucy's Lab allows her to be the scientist she always wanted to be.

About the Illustrator

Elizabeth Zechel is an illustrator and author of the children's book *Is There a Mouse in the Baby's Room?* Her illustrations appear in books such as *Wordbirds* by Liesl Schillinger, *The Little General and the Giant Snowflake* by Matthea Harvey, and cookbooks such as *Bubby's Homemade Pies* by Jen Bervin and Ron Silver, as well as a variety of magazine and literary journals. She lives in Brooklyn, NY where she teaches Kindergarten.